STORYTIME COLLECTION

STORYTIME COLLECTION

This book belongs to

_____

_____

Autumn
Publishing

Published in 2020
by Autumn Publishing
Cottage Farm
Sywell
NN6 0BJ
www.igloobooks.com

0920 004
6 8 10 12 11 9 7 5
ISBN 978-1-78810-995-6

Printed and manufactured in China

Disney
THE JUNGLE BOOK

🌿 STORYTIME COLLECTION 🌿

Long ago, deep in the Indian jungle, Bagheera, a wise and caring black panther, was walking along the side of the river. There, he came across a boat that had crashed onto the shore. Inside was a baby in a basket. "It's a Man-cub," said Bagheera to himself.

Bagheera knew the Man-cub needed
food and care, but the nearest Man-village
was days away. Instead, he hoped to leave the baby
with a mother wolf who had recently given birth to
a litter of cubs. She was very happy to accept the
Man-cub as one of her own.

Ten years passed and the Man-cub, who became known as Mowgli, lived happily with the wolves.

As well as his wolf pack family, Mowgli was also popular with other animals in the jungle. There was one, however, who didn't like the boy one bit.

His name was Shere Khan, a strong and cunning tiger, feared throughout the jungle.

Shere Khan was afraid Mowgli would grow up to become a hunter and vowed to make sure this never happened.

Fearing for Mowgli's life, and that of the pack,
Akela, the leader of the wolves, called a meeting.
"Shere Khan will surely kill the boy and all who
try to protect him," he declared. So, for the good
of the pack, the decision was made that Mowgli
should no longer be allowed to stay.

When Rama, Mowgli's wolf father, was told the news, he was very upset. "The boy cannot survive alone in the jungle!" he cried.

Bagheera, who had come to check up on Mowgli, had been listening to the wolves talking and came up with an idea to help. "I know a Man-village where Mowgli would be safe," he said. "I'm sure he'll go with me."

"So be it," replied Akela. "There is no time to lose."

Early next morning, without telling the boy why, Bagheera took Mowgli away. Even with the child on his back, he moved swiftly and the two were soon deep in the jungle.

As night-time came, Mowgli started to feel sleepy. "Shouldn't we go back home?" he asked.

"We're not going back," replied Bagheera. "I'm taking you to a Man-village."

Mowgli tried to protest, but Bagheera
refused to listen. It was time to sleep and he
was looking for a safe place for them both.
The panther finally found a tall tree they could use.

"Go on," he said, "up you go." Once they were both
safely on the thick branch, Bagheera lay down and closed
his eyes.

The panther was soon sound asleep, leaving a sad Mowgli
to think about all the jungle friends he would be leaving
behind. Neither of them noticed Kaa, a large, slithering
snake, appear above them.

"S-s-say now, what have we here?" asked Kaa.
"It's a Man-cub. A delicious Man-cub."

"Oh, go away and leave me alone," said Mowgli.
He tried to push Kaa away with his hand, but the
snake didn't leave. Instead, he began to hypnotise
Mowgli using his large, scary eyes. "Sleep little
Man-cub," hissed Kaa. "Rest in peace."

As Mowgli drifted off to sleep, Kaa began
to coil himself around the helpless young
boy. Then, the snake opened his mouth as wide as it
would go, as his head moved closer to Mowgli.

Suddenly, Bagheera woke up and saw what was happening.
"Hold it, Kaa!" he cried. The panther leapt forward and
batted the snake with his large, black paw. Kaa released
Mowgli from his grip and turned to attack Bagheera.

"You have just made a s-s-serious mistake, my friend," hissed Kaa, who began to hypnotise the panther. But before he could coil himself around Bagheera, Mowgli, who had woken from his trance, pushed Kaa off the branch. Finally defeated, a hungry Kaa slithered off into the depths of the jungle.

The next morning, after a good night's sleep,
the pair were woken by a loud rumbling sound from
below. "A parade!" called out Mowgli, excitedly.

Bagheera covered his ears. "Oh, no," he said,
groaning. "The dawn patrol."

Mowgli grabbed a vine and swung down from
the tree to take a look.

Mowgli watched as a long line of elephants marched proudly in single file.
He ran over to a baby elephant that marched at the back of the line.
"What are you doing?" asked Mowgli.

"Drilling," replied the baby elephant.

"Can I do it, too?" asked Mowgli.

"Sure," said the baby elephant.
"Just do what I do."

Mowgli got in step behind the baby elephant and began to march on all fours. Suddenly, Colonel Hathi, who was leading the patrol, called out, "TO THE REAR, MARCH!"

Not knowing this meant he had to turn around, Mowgli bumped right into the baby elephant.

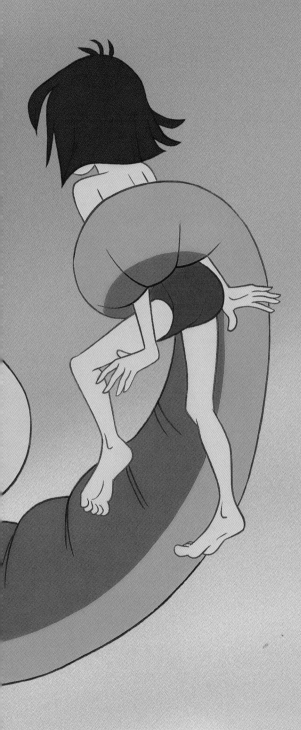

"COMPANY, HALT!" cried Colonel
Hathi. All the elephants stopped,
ready for inspection. It didn't take
long for Hathi to notice Mowgli.
"I'll have no Man-cub in my jungle!"
he cried, as he picked Mowgli up
with his trunk.

"It's not your jungle," replied Mowgli.

Bagheera quickly rushed down to speak to Hathi. "The Man-cub is with me," he said. "I'm taking him to the Man-village."

"To stay?" asked Hathi.

"You have the word of Bagheera," replied the panther.

"Good," said the grumpy elephant, who turned away and marched off with the rest of the herd.

Bagheera turned to Mowgli. "You're going to the Man-village, right now," he said.

"I'm not going!" cried the boy. "I'm staying here." With that, he grabbed hold of the nearest tree and refused to let go.

"You're going if I have to drag you!" shouted Bagheera, who tried in vain to pull him off the tree. The panther quickly lost his temper. "I've had it, Man-cub. From now on, you're on your own."

Now all alone, Mowgli wandered through the jungle. Suddenly, a bear called Baloo walked by, singing and dancing happily.

"Well, now, what have we here?" asked Baloo, when he saw Mowgli.

"Go away," replied the boy, who was still upset after his fight with Bagheera.

But Baloo wouldn't go away and, instead, offered to teach Mowgli about the bare necessities of life in the jungle. He taught him how to fight like a bear, as well as how to find bananas and other foods. The whole time, Baloo was singing and dancing, and the Man-cub soon felt much happier.

A few days later, Mowgli and Baloo were singing as they floated down the river. "I like being a bear," said Mowgli.

"You make one swell bear," said Baloo. "Why, you even sing like one."

Out of nowhere, a group of monkeys
appeared and snatched the Man-cub from
off Baloo's belly. "Hey!" cried Mowgli.
"Let go of me!"

No matter how hard he struggled against the
chuckling monkeys, Mowgli couldn't get free.

Baloo shook an angry fist at the monkeys.
"Give me back my Man-cub!" he demanded.

"Come and get him," said the laughing monkeys,
who picked fruit from off the trees and threw it at Baloo.

Then, the monkeys quickly carried Mowgli away, but Baloo had an idea. "Bagheera!" he cried, hoping the panther was still close.

Fortunately, Bagheera heard the cry and came running. He asked Baloo where Mowgli was and the bear replied, "The mangy monkeys carried him off."

Bagheera knew the monkeys would have taken Mowgli to the ancient ruins, as that was where King Louie, the leader of the monkeys, lived. Wasting no more time, the bear and panther set off to rescue their friend.

Meanwhile, at the ancient ruins, Mowgli was introduced to King Louie. The king had heard that Mowgli wanted to stay in the jungle and offered to help the Man-cub. But he wanted something in return. "I wanna be like you-oo-oo," said King Louie, believing Mowgli knew how to make fire.

"I don't know how to make fire," replied Mowgli.

King Louie didn't believe him.

Bagheera and Baloo arrived soon after and the panther quickly came up with a plan. "While you create a disturbance," he said to Baloo, "I'll rescue Mowgli."

With that, Baloo disguised himself to distract the king of the monkeys.

As Baloo and King Louie were dancing,
Bagheera tried to rescue Mowgli.

Despite the monkeys guarding the boy,
the cunning panther was able to grab his
friend and the two of them escaped,
with Baloo, back into the jungle.

That night, as Mowgli slept, Bagheera explained to Baloo why the boy had to be taken to the Man-village. "Sooner or later, Mowgli will meet Shere Khan," said Bagheera. Despite how much Baloo loved having his friend around, he knew Mowgli wouldn't be safe as long as that terrible tiger was after him.

When morning came, and Mowgli was awake, Baloo spoke to him. "I've got to take you to the Man-village," he said, reluctantly.

Not wanting to leave the jungle, Mowgli ran off, only to fall into Kaa's clutches once more! "Nice to s-s-see you again," hissed the snake.

Shere Khan, who believed Mowgli was close by, heard Kaa talking and tugged on the snake's tail to get his attention. "I'd like a word with you," purred Shere Khan, as he revealed his long, sharp claws. "Forgive me if I've interrupted anything."

"Oh no, nothing at all," lied Kaa, who didn't want the tiger to take Mowgli away from him.

While the tiger and snake were talking, Mowgli managed to escape from Kaa's coils. He ran away once more, feeling more alone than ever.

After travelling for a long time, Mowgli arrived at an area where there was no grass on the ground, or leaves on the trees. Soon, four vultures joined him. "He's got legs like a stork," said one.

"But he ain't got no feathers," said another.

All the vultures laughed at poor Mowgli, until they saw how sad the Man-cub really was.

Instead of teasing, the vultures decided to try and cheer Mowgli up. "Kid, we'd like to make you an honorary vulture," they said.

"I'd rather be on my own," said Mowgli.

"Now look, kid, everybody's got to have friends," said one vulture. Suddenly, all four started singing and dancing. "We're your friends, we're your friends," they all sang.

Mowgli was soon smiling and dancing along.

Unknown to Mowgli and the vultures, Shere Khan was nearby.
He heard the vultures singing and went over to investigate.
As the song finished he spoke. "Bravo," he sneered.
"And thank you for detaining my victim."

Frightened by Shere Khan, the vultures flew off. From the
safety of a tree, they urged Mowgli to run.

Mowgli refused. "You don't scare me," he said to Shere Khan.

"You have spirit," said the tiger. "Spirit deserving of a sporting chance. I am going to count to ten."

But Mowgli still didn't run. Shere Khan finished counting and leapt at Mowgli, only for Baloo to arrive in the nick of time and grab the tiger by his tail.

The vultures and Baloo fought Shere Khan, but he was too strong for them. Suddenly, lightning struck an old tree, causing it to burst into flames. "Fire!" cried one of the vultures. "It's the only thing old stripes is afraid of!"

Mowgli grabbed a burning branch and tied it to Shere Khan's tail. Terrified by the piece of burning wood attached to his body, Shere Khan ran away, never to be seen again. "Good old papa bear!" cried Mowgli, as he thanked Baloo for saving his life.

Realising it was time to leave the jungle for good, Mowgli
let Baloo and Bagheera take him to the Man-village.
When they arrived, the young boy heard a girl singing.
He couldn't take his eyes off her. When the young girl
saw Mowgli, she smiled at him.

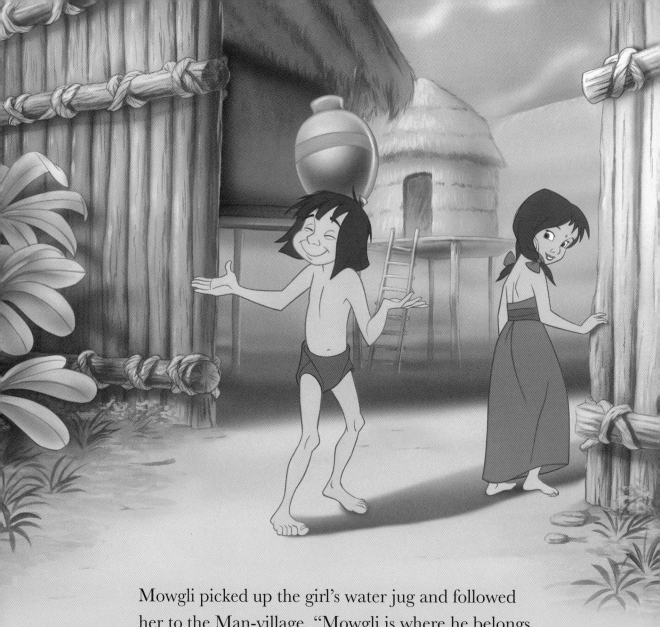

Mowgli picked up the girl's water jug and followed
her to the Man-village. "Mowgli is where he belongs
now," said Bagheera.

"I think you're right," said Baloo.

The pair watched as Mowgli turned around and
gave them both one last, happy smile, before
heading inside, where he lived happily ever after.

COLLECT THEM ALL!

With 7 more exciting titles to choose from, you'll want to complete your Storytime Collection!

How far will a father go for his son?

Will Rapunzel learn who she truly is?

Will Moana be able to save the ocean?

Can Anna and Elsa stop an eternal winter?

Will Simba ever become king?

Will the Incredibles save the day?

Will Belle be able to break the curse?